DON'T BE SILLY, MRS. MILLIE!

by Judy Cox

illustrated by Joe Mathieu

Marshall Cavendish

New York London Singapore

Marshall Cavendish, 99 White Plains Road, Tarrytown, NY 10591
www.marshallcavendish.us

Library of Congress Cataloging-in-Publication Data
Cox, Judy.
Don't be silly, Mrs. Millie!/Judy Cox; illustrated by Joe Mathieu.—1st ed.
p. cm.
Summary: A teacher makes her students laugh when she mixes up words, saying "goats"
instead of "coats" and "poodles" when she means "puddles."
ISBN-13: 978-0-7614-5166-2
ISBN-10: 0-7614-5166-8
[1.Teachers—Fiction. 2. Schools—Fiction. 3. Humorous stories.] Don't Be Silly, Mrs. Millie!.
II. Mathieu, Joseph, ill. III. Title.
PZ7.C83835Do 2005
[E]—dc21
2004019320

The text of this book is set in Century Schoolbook.
The illustrations are rendered in Prismacolor pencil, dyes, pen, and ink.
Book design by Adam Mietlowski

Printed in China

First edition
4 6 5

To my students, who inspire me every day
—J. C.

To my daughter, Kristen
—J. M.

MRS. MILLIE, our teacher, is really silly.

Every day she says, "Good morning, children.
Please hang up your goats."
"Don't be silly, Mrs. Millie! You mean our coats!"

At eight o'clock our teacher announces, "Please rise for the frog salute."

"Oh, no," we shout. "You mean the flag salute!"

"It's nine o'clock. Time to write," Mrs. Millie says. "Get out your paper and penguins."

"Don't be silly, Mrs. Millie! You mean our paper and pencils!"

At ten o'clock it's recess time. Our teacher looks out the window. "It just stopped raining cats and dogs. Don't step in a poodle!"

"Don't you mean a puddle?" we ask, giggling.

We play outside until our teacher blows her whistle.
"Recess is over," she yells. "It's time to chameleon!"
"Don't be silly, Mrs. Millie! You mean it's time to come in."

At eleven o'clock Mrs. Millie says,
"You may get drinks, but don't cut in the lion."
"You mean the line!" we yell.

At twelve o'clock our teacher announces, "Time for lunch. Wash your hands with soap and walrus."
"You're silly, Mrs. Millie! You mean soap and water."

As we get in line, Mrs. Millie reminds us, "Don't forget your lunch bunny."

"Oh, that's right, our lunch money!" we shout.

Mrs. Millie puts on her glasses to read the menu. "They have gorilla cheese sandwiches today."

"Don't be silly, Mrs. Millie! You mean grilled cheese sandwiches!"

At one o'clock our teacher picks up a book.
"It's story time. Come sit on the bug."

"You're so silly!" we cry. "You mean sit on the rug."

At two o'clock Mrs. Millie calls us to the back of the room. "It's time for Art. Who wants to paint on the weasel?"

"You mean the easel, Mrs. Millie! How can you be so silly?" we ask.

After Art our teacher asks, "Who's hungry?
We have parrot sticks and quackers."

"We know what you mean—carrot sticks and crackers!" we yell.

At three o'clock Mrs. Millie smiles. "What a fun day we've had! But it's time to go home. Put on your bats and kittens."

"Don't be silly, Mrs. Millie! You mean our hats and mittens!"

When we're ready to leave, our teacher goes to the door. "Butterfly, children."

"No, Mrs. Millie," we shout. "You don't mean butterfly. You mean good-bye!"
Mrs. Millie laughs. We laugh too.
"Butterfly, Mrs. Millie. See you gator!"

And we wave good-bye as we get on the octopus.